The Memory Box

SARAH VENESS

Also available in large print and Kindle editions.

ISBN: 1-9734-8655-5

ISBN-13: 978-1-9734-8655-8

DEDICATION

To everyone who fears the dark:

'Don't curse the darkness – light a candle'

CONTENTS

ACKNOWLEDGMENTS

I want to take this opportunity to thank all my friends, actual and virtual, who have encouraged me to find my voice and then been prepared to listen.

THE INNER SONG

Kate had been quietly listening to the inner song that was playing in Freda's heart and mind.

For the last few months she had been visiting Freda in her flat, which now showed signs of neglect and abandonment. Once house-proud, she would never have let the cobwebs string their way from the light fitting to the picture rail, and the curtains would have been pulled back to let in as much light as possible. Her confidence was seeping away, it was as if she had drawn the curtains in her mind and inside the house an unheard story was being enacted.

Kate enjoyed hearing stories of Freda's past, but it had been hard work coaxing her to communicate recently, as she had become subdued and depressed. Any mention of activity met with a negative response. Kate's idea of getting her to a reminiscence group had become a distant dream.

Never one to give in easily, Kate would occasionally mention the group that met in the Black Cat Café and what lovely cakes they had there. Freda's sweet tooth competed with her fear of the future and the dread of the past.

It was a spring day when Freda agreed to go with Kate. 'Just to have a look at the cakes.' They set off in the gentle sunshine, Freda's stick tappity-tapping on the pavement. The café was only a short walk away. Outside it didn't look much, but inside it was clean and the food was good.

Barry and Audrey were regulars who had commandeered the sofa, and Ted was at the counter trying to decide which cake to have. Kate motioned to Freda to pull up a chair and said she would order the drinks and cakes. 'Have a look at the menu and let me know what you fancy – the hot chocolate with marshmallows is superb.' Raising her voice barely above a whisper Freda asked for a hot chocolate and an éclair.

The café bell rang as another customer came in. 'Hi John' called Audrey, 'good to see you again. How's your knee after the op?' John leant heavily on his stick, 'Fine I'm doing fine, it's good to get out again.' He made his way over to the armchair next to the sofa, and motioned to Stan the owner, 'Cup of the usual, Stan, and a bacon butty.'

Kate returned to table and, as she handed her the éclair, she introduced Freda to the group. Freda liked the café, it was warm and homely, and more pleasant than she had expected. She and Kate sat a little away from the group that was now forming, close enough to hear their conversations but keeping their distance.

Ted had finally settled on a vanilla slice and joined the others, lowering his bulky frame into a vacant chair.

Barry decided to get the ball rolling and asked if anyone would like to share any memories from their childhood.

Audrey said she had learnt to knit when she was four, and had built on the skill all her life. She nodded in the direction of Barry, who was modelling her latest hand-knitted creation – a Fair Isle pullover.

Patting his jumper fondly, Barry launched into his boyhood love of cricket. 'I played in the village cricket team using my Dad's bat. which was almost as big as I was. The pitch seemed so big then, and I dreamed of scoring a century, but I never made more than seven runs before I got bowled out.'

Ted joined in, 'The teas were the best bit of our cricket matches.' If you asked Ted what his hobby was, he would have to admit it was eating, and by the look of him he had been practising all his life.

His mind went back to the happy days when he prayed for bad light or rain to stop play during a match, and he could return to the clubhouse early, and tuck into the amazing array of bread and cakes. 'I really enjoyed the sandwiches – the sausage ones were best, followed by ham and tomato, egg and cress, cheese and pickle.' Ted's eyes glowed and he was smacking his lips as he continued. 'They were followed by scones and jam, marble cake, and wonderful Victoria sponges which were about a foot high and oozing with jam and cream.'

He had brought a selection of sweets from the Olde Sweet Shop in town with him. He had been a customer for 60 years and whatever else he had lost – his hair, his hearing – his sweet tooth remained intact.

He offered the paper bag around the group, leaning towards Kate and Freda to include them in his act of generosity.

Barry then was reminded of buying sweets when he was a boy. 'When I was a lad I used to walk from our cottage to the nearest shop, which was half a mile away, but it was always worth it. As I walked along the road, gripping my sixpenny piece tightly in my fist, I'd be planning what I would spend the money on. Sometimes it was really hard not to eat all the sweets before I got home.'

Barry then remembered something else. 'The Suffolk village where we lived was very remote, with just one weekly bus to Norwich, but on Sunday afternoons a mobile shop used to come to our village. A car would hoot its horn and we would rush out from our cottage, almost taking the gate off its hinges in our excitement. In the boot were the Sunday papers and comics and boxes of confectionery. We jostled with the neighbours, and then went back to relax and enjoy our purchases. I can still remember reading The Beano and sucking everlasting toffees in the drowsy summer sunshine. Life seemed perfect then.'

'But it wasn't,' interrupted Audrey 'I remember you complaining about the outside lavvy. You told me it smelt in summer and you froze in the winter.'

Freda tilted her body towards the group, edging slightly closer, but with her arms tightly folded across her chest, not wanting to be included, but afraid of missing out on something.

John shifted his leg to alleviate the pain. 'My Mother was a wonderful singer. She sang in the church choir on a Sunday, and in a choral society on a Wednesday night. I used to love hearing her practice.' He paused to change position again, 'Sadly I didn't inherit her singing voice, but I did get her good looks!'

Laughter rippled around the room. Freda smiled, and Kate was pleased to see her respond. Audrey then said 'When I was a young girl we lived near the seaside, at Leigh-on-Sea. It was lovely! We used to play on the mounds of cockle shells, and when the tide was out we would run across the mud to paddle in a tiny little river called the Ray'.

Freda imagined the scene, and the smell of ozone was almost tangible. In her mind she could hear her mother and aunt singing 'I do love to be beside the seaside', their skirts tucked into the legs of their bloomers as they paddled in the sea, giggling, forgetting how starved of pleasure their day- to-day lives had become. 'Well, Kate, would you or your friend like to share anything?'

Barry was keen to give Freda an opportunity to share if she wanted to. Kate was unsure whether Freda would rise to the occasion, as there was no pressure to take part. Freda kept quiet, so she launched into sharing some of her own memories. 'I travelled between my estranged parents and their various partners. Mum lived in rural Berkshire and my Dad lived in the East End of London. We liked it when Dad took us to the museums and art galleries. I didn't fit into the horsey scene in Berkshire. I had no desire to ride, and mucking out would have been my worst nightmare. I retreated into a world of books. That's why I became a librarian. Books were my best friends.'

Freda's own childhood had been filled with love, despite living from hand to mouth. Without thinking she suddenly said, 'One day my dad took my brother Bill and me to Petticoat Lane and we went to Kossoff's bakery and we bought jam doughnuts and the jam oozed out when I bit into it and trickled down onto my leg.'

Ted looked up at the mention of doughnuts. 'My grandfather bought me a doughnut for breakfast once, I never forgot his kindness.'

The conversations then continued along the subject of food until Barry called a halt and asked for suggestions of themes for next week. A few ideas were put forward, including, 'Games We Used to Play' from Audrey, 'Old Films' from John, School Dinners from Ted, but it was decided that everyone would bring a photo from their past, and tell the group what it meant to them.

Freda was feeling so much brighter. By the time she came to leave her mood had lifted, and she was already turning over in her mind what photograph to bring next week.

TASTE OF THE SECRET

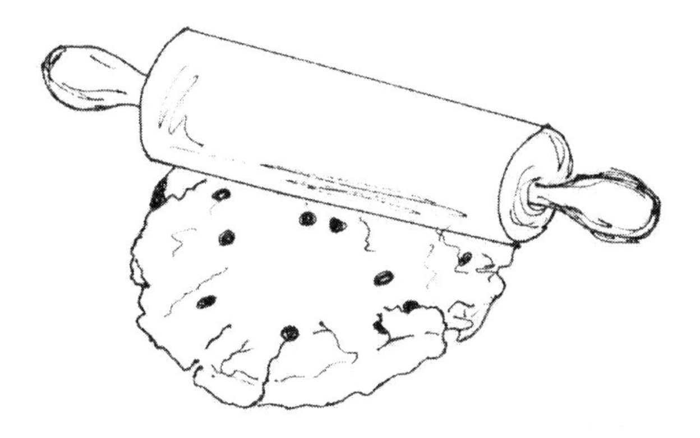

The sun streamed through the kitchen window and was filtered by the curtain of flour falling silently from the sieve.

As she sifted the flour and baking powder for the third time, Sally could hear her mother's voice saying, 'Incorporate lots of air as you sieve it'. Sally had inherited her mother Elizabeth's love of cooking, and thought back to the warmth and security she had felt as she watched her mother baking in their small kitchen, with its red floor tiles which she religiously buffed up to a shine every Friday with Cardinal Polish.

This was the kitchen where Sally played happily at the sturdy drop-leaf table, transforming the pictures in her colouring book into works of art (which would be given to relatives and friends to display briefly on their walls) while her mother cooked all manner of dishes.

The smell of baking filtered around the house, and Sally started to rub the fat into the flour of the family's favourite – fruit scones. Her fingertips rose repeatedly to a height of at least nine inches, to get in as much air as possible. She couldn't count how many times she had watched her mother go through this familiar routine.

Mealtimes were sacred. Not like today's 'Eat and Run' culture. They never ate meals from a tray in front of the TV in those days – the table was always laid with the best cutlery, including fish knives and forks on a Friday. Not that they were Catholic, but it was just the routine of life that Friday was fish day, Sunday was roast day, and Monday was when the left-over meat was minced and made into shepherd's pie – or spaghetti bolognaise if her mother was feeling adventurous.

Sally poured the milk slowly into the crumbed mix and stirred it in. 'Don't overhandle it' Elizabeth's instructions rang in her ears 'You will know you have the right consistency when the scone mix picks up all the crumbs from the side of the bowl. If it's too dry, add a splash more milk. Just a splash, mind – not too much. If it's too wet, add some more flour.'

Then she gently shaped all the ingredients into a smooth round form, taking care not to over-work it. A dusting of flour was scattered onto the board and, picking up Elizabeth's cherished wooden rolling pin, she began to roll out the scone mix.

She remembered the day her father arrived home with a marble rolling pin and gave it to her mother, extolling its virtues. He explained that in the olden days those marble eggs, which you now see in gift shops, weren't just for decoration. Victorian cooks would roll them in their hands to keep them cool, which in turn meant the pastry would hold its flavour. A marble rolling pin, in his opinion, was the best you could get, and her mother had done her best to look pleased at this unexpected and unwelcome gift. He had found it in a junk shop and was convinced that it would improve her baking, though she didn't think there was anything lacking in the first place.

Elizabeth had said she couldn't use it straight away, as she wanted to make sure it was scrupulously clean before letting it anywhere near her pastry, and promptly put it into a bowl of bleach. Crestfallen, her father walked through the kitchen and out to his shed to lick his wounds.

When the next time came to do some more baking, her mother dusted the marble rolling pin with flour to make it look as if it had been put to good service, but she actually used the old wooden one she has inherited from her mother. This activity was like a sacrament to her, a visible sign of invisible grace, as her rolling pin had its own history. It had been passed down through the generations – before her mother owned it, it had belonged to her grandmother, and probably her great grandmother too. She felt warm inside, knowing that her hands were holding the same round handles as her forbears, performing the same familiar tasks with equal love.

Sally's mind wandered back to her grandmother's kitchen. It had been practical, homely, and very well-used. The legendary scrubbed pine table, under which her uncle Tony had been born during an air raid, was the focus of the kitchen. The table's fame went even further back than that. In 1902 – the year that King Edward the Seventh had his appendix operation – her Great Aunt Elsie had the same procedure a week later. Being too ill to be moved to hospital, the surgeon operated right in her own home, and Sally's great grandmother always said the kitchen table top, in its new role as an operating table, was where Elsie's life was saved.

The yellow kitchen larder unit was Granny's pride and joy, with its drop-down work surface and Art Deco handles. The weighing scales with the tiny weights were a source of much delight to little Sally, and she had spent many a happy hour getting them to balance. She didn't mind what she weighed – getting them equal was what gave her great pleasure.

For years she had been under the misapprehension that flapjacks were so named because Granny always kept them in the larder cabinet. When she let the flap down, there they would be sitting, golden and sweet, on a tea plate, just waiting for a hungry young girl to enjoy. Sally would breathe deeply, savouring the smell of the treacle before taking her first delicious oaty bite. Even now she could conjure up the smell and the taste, her mouth-watering at the memory, her fingers almost feeling the coarseness of the oats. She found memory an amazing thing – sometimes whole chunks seem to be missing, and then one small reminder opens up a treasure trove where buried memories lie.

As she looked at the sugar canister on the work top, her mind travelled back to the day her mother had put some transfers of red cherries on her glass storage jars. She was so proud of what she had done. Sally pictured the glass sugar jar with its red lid and the vanilla pod that flavoured the sugar with its floral earthy smell, and remembered the look of happiness on Elizabeth's face.

Grinning, she remembered the saga of the marble rolling pin. Rolling out the dough, she carefully rolled up from the middle, and then down from the middle. Turning the dough ninety degrees each time, she continued to roll it, until it measured an inch thick. Pastry cutter in hand, she then stamped out the rounds and placed them onto the baking tray.

Her father had been most insistent that the marble rolling pin was the bee's knees when it came to baking, and every time her mother baked, he would say how much better everything tasted since she had had it. Little did he know that never, ever, not even once, did she use it, because she loved the connection with the past that came from handling her wooden heirloom.

Her father would eye up his wife's pastry like a master chef, admiring its colour and texture, and as he tasted the first mouthful would exclaim. 'Very good pastry, Lizzie. All the better for the marble rolling pin.' and with a satisfied smile would munch his way through whatever she put in front of him.

Sally brushed egg and milk onto the scones, just as her mother had taught her, then popped them in the oven. When they were golden brown, and an enticing aroma wafted through the house, the back door opened and in walked her father. He sniffed the air and said, 'This smell takes me back! Your mother was a wonderful baker. I guess you still use her marble rolling pin? Her cooking really took an upturn when I bought it for her.'

Sally raised her eyes to heaven and a warm feeling flowed through her. She smiled – some secrets are best never shared.

THE SHED

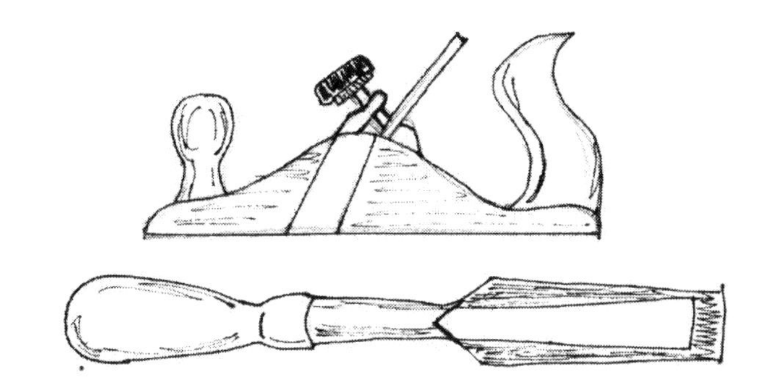

Richard's fingers turned the screws that lay in the sawdust speckled-tin and then his hands surreptitiously slid across the workbench towards the chisel. There amongst the bird seed, the curly wood shavings, and the saddle soap left over from when he went riding, his mind went back to happier days.

Here was the place that he retreated to when Elizabeth and her mother bickered over the pronunciation of the word 'almond' or 'clematis', – somewhere to smoke his pipe and turn wood on his lathe. It had been his place of reprieve and respite from the pressing world of finance before he retired, but now it seemed like a void – a vacuum which needed filling again.

The lathe had lain redundant after Elizabeth died, cobwebs hung at the windows like miniature trampolines for spiders to play on, and the shelves was full of the dust of the years.

Next to the lathe, linseed oil and tins of varnish jostled for position on a small tray that Elizabeth had made herself. He ran his fingers over the basket work, and remembered her hands moving repetitiously and rhythmically as she wove the reeds. This tray was the first of several she had completed, and he stroked its oval birch base, treasuring the memory of the Christmas morning when he unwrapped the strangely-shaped package.

She would bring his drinks and cake out to the shed on it, and he realised he wanted to start using it again. Although there were no more homemade cakes, bourbon biscuits and chocolate digestives would be fine. He removed the varnish and bottle of linseed oil and put them on the shelf amongst the other tools of his trade.

Becoming Elizabeth's carer was not how he had imagined their retirement would be spent. They had had so many hopes and dreams. Together they had planned excursions to far flung places – a cruise to see the Northern Lights, a trip to see the Taj Mahal. They had both been keen to learn new skills – Elizabeth fancied learning Italian, while Richard wanted to learn to speak Tamil, to cook authentic curries, and to have more time to do his wood turning.

Retirement was something he had looked forward to, and they had they been counting down the days for years, but after enjoying it for only three months, Elizabeth was diagnosed with cancer.

She was incredibly courageous, and he had put on a brave face, but when he came out to the shed and was out of earshot, he would weep.

The next eighteen months were a roller-coaster emotionally as well as physically. She would have good and bad days and downright difficult ones. They both resented the intrusion the illness had made into their lives – life seemed to revolve around hospital appointments and treatments. They had tried alternative therapies and all manner of weird and wonderful diets, but there was no getting away from it, she was disappearing in front of his eyes like the setting sun. Little by little she sank lower, until all that was left was the warm glow you get before nightfall, and he knew that complete darkness would soon envelop him.

He spent less and less time in the shed as she deteriorated, only snatching a few minutes respite here and there when she was dozing, but this was the place where he felt safe to let out his emotions and catch his breath.

When she died he couldn't face going in there. The place, which once had been like a cocoon of solace, became as unfriendly as a tomb. Numbed, his emotions became as solid as a block of ice.

The promise of Spring, with leaves unfurling in the watery sunshine, began a melting in his heart, too. He knew that the last thing Elizabeth would have wanted was for him to become insular and emotionally detached. Slowly he began to thaw out, but the shed remained like a symbol of his empty, aching heart.

It had seemed a prolonged winter, and it was now six months since Elizabeth had died. Although he knew time had passed at its usual rate, the months had seemed longer than in previous years.

Pulling on a fleece, he ventured into the garden to admire the Clematis Armandii, which was climbing over the shed, and caught a whiff of its vanilla scent. A faint smile crossed his face when he remembered Elizabeth and her mother arguing over the pronunciation of its name.

Peering through the window, amidst the dust, he looked at the chisel that he had thrown down in haste on the bench when he had heard Elizabeth cry out in pain. There it had lain, untouched and neglected since that day. Normally it would have been wiped with an oily rag and returned to its proper place amongst the other chisels that were lined up in a row, like soldiers on parade, ready to be used again.

Reflected in the glass of the window he could see behind him the cherry tree, flushed with pink blossom – a short-lived and bittersweet reminder of happier days. It was as if Elizabeth was speaking to him through the beauty of the tree, urging him to go into the shed, in this new season of his life.

He turned with a decisiveness that surprised him, and went into the house to collect the padlock key.

His hands shook as he put the key into the lock. It was stiff to open, after its long winter of abandonment, but it finally turned. As the door opened, a musty smell of mildew and mould and rancid birdseed reached his nostrils, but specks of dust rose into the air as he entered through the doorway, and his heart lifted with them and the odour of opportunity filled the atmosphere.

No longer an empty tomb, the shed welcomed him, enveloping him with a sense of resurrection and hope. Ashes to ashes, dust to dust, his love for Elizabeth would live on and never die. Here he felt a new closeness to her, as if she had been waiting for him to open the door of his heart.

Touching the handle of the chisel, he knew it was time to carve himself a new future.

I watched as Daisy made her way to her grandmother and clambered onto her lap. Her tears had stopped and now she felt safe in the old chintz chair, with Granny's kindly arms enveloping her with warmth and love. They made eye contact and my mother wiped away the last remaining tear from Daisy's cheek.

'Falling over is just part of growing up, Daisy – everyone has done it. I can remember falling over in the playground at school when my foot got caught in a skipping rope, and Mummy was always falling over when she was your age. So come along now, no more crying.'

'Can you tell me a story Granny?' Daisy asked, as she made herself comfortable, smiling through her tears. She took hold of the spinning wheel on her grandmother's bracelet between her chubby fingers and looked at it curiously. 'What's this?' she asked, and my mother looked at the charm on her silver bracelet and began to tell the story.

'This is a spinning wheel and it comes from Wales, which was where I met Grandpa when I was nineteen. I was working in the bakery in our village, and the first time he walked in I was up to my elbows in dough, making Eccles cakes.

He loved cake and he started to pop in regularly to buy buns and Welsh cakes. He was very handsome, with his thick black hair and tanned skin. He worked on his parent's farm in the next valley, milking the cows and looking after the sheep. His cheeks were always red – just like yours.

One day he sauntered in and, as he paid me for the cake, he leaned forwards and asked 'Would you like to come with me to the dance hall on Saturday?' and his cheeks flamed even redder than usual. I shyly nodded and before I knew it, I had said 'Yes.'

On Saturday evening he arrived at our cottage, his hair slicked back with Brilliantine and his usually mud-stained hands looking as if he had bleached them for the occasion. His boots were highly polished, and he had put on clean clothes. I wore my best dress and my white sandals, with my hair piled up on my head.

This was the first of many dates we had before we got married. Grandpa's mother used to spin the wool from the sheep, and when we got engaged he bought me this silver bracelet and the spinning wheel charm.'

'And this one, Granny, tell me about this one.' Daisy shifted position and the Heart charm was now cradled in her little hand.

'He gave me this heart on our wedding day, I was very surprised, as he wasn't a very demonstrative man. I bought him a signet ring and he wore it every day for the rest of his life. He did look smart at the wedding in his suit, with a paisley tie and shiny shoes.

I wore a simple sky-blue polka dot dress with a deep white belt and white collar. I didn't want to spend money on a traditional wedding dress as I wanted to save money towards our life together, and so chose something that could be worn more than once.

We weren't rich, so we used freshly-picked wild flowers and cow parsley in glass milk bottles to decorate the tables. My bouquet was a bunch of sunflowers and I had the prettiest shoes you ever saw.

Daisy looked down at her pink shoes with their butterflies and flowers embroidered on them and couldn't believe that Granny's wedding shoes could be as nice as hers. I watched my mother's eyes glisten and sparkle as she thought back to that day. Where had the time gone?

'Granny, what's this?'

'That, my poppet, is a sunflower. Just like the ones I had in my wedding bouquet. When we had been married for a whole year, Grandpa gave the charm to me as an anniversary present. He was such a kind man. '

She turned the silver chain round in her fingers and fingered another charm. 'This one is a Vespa scooter. When we had our very first holiday abroad, Grandpa and I went to Italy and we rode on one of these.' A smile crept across her face and her unfocused gaze made me realise she was reliving the holiday of her youth.

I smiled, imagining my parents looking like Audrey Hepburn and Gregory Peck in the film 'Roman Holiday'. What a gay and giddy holiday it must have been, full of innocence and magic as they rode around on the scooter – Mum with her hair flying free in the wind. Then sitting in a roadside cafe eating ice cream, enjoying watching the world go by – such luxury compared to their hard work on the farm.

Mum told me I was conceived on that holiday in Florence, and they thought about naming me after the city, but Daddy had a Great Aunt Florence who was a very difficult woman – always muttering to herself under her breath and sitting with her arms tightly crossed over her chest. He said nothing would induce him to inflict such a name on his firstborn, so he chose Deborah instead, which means 'like a bee – unselfish, humble and untiring'. Much better attributes than those of his ghastly Great Aunt, and that is how the silver bee charm made its way onto the bracelet.

'Oh Granny, why have you got a butterfly on the bracelet? I love butterflies! They are so pretty, see I've got one on my shoe'.

'When your Auntie Vanessa was born we spent ages thinking of nice names for her. I liked Megan or Dorothy, and Grandpa liked Charlotte or Susan, we just couldn't make up our minds. One evening we were watching the television and a beautiful young actress called Vanessa Redgrave came on the screen and we looked at each other and knew we had found the perfect name for our dainty little child.

When we looked it up in the book that told you what baby names mean, we found out it meant butterfly, and we knew then that we had made the right choice. Grandpa then got me a silver butterfly to add to my collection.'

'Do you know what this charm is, Daisy? It's a sewing machine, because I used to make all Mummy's and Auntie Vanessa's dresses. I made you some lovely clothes, didn't I, Deborah?'

'Yes, Mum, they were wonderful. We never had the same clothes as the people who bought theirs at the shops.'

I remembered so well lying in my bed in the soft summer evening light, hearing the gentle sound of the bees buzzing in the flower beds underneath my window, punctuated by the 'chukka chukka chukka' of the sewing machine needle going through the cloth.

I watched the love flowing between Daisy and my Mum. I picked up my mobile and went out into the conservatory to ring Vanessa. After a minute or so she answered.

'Hi Debs, is everything OK? You don't usually ring me during the day.'

'I think may now be the perfect time to tell Mum. Are you free this afternoon?'

'As it happens I am only ten minutes away, as I've just been to a difficult birth at Grigg's Farm, but I'm not dressed for afternoon tea!'

'That's ok, as I'm not dressed for it either! I've been gardening with Mum and Daisy. That is, until she fell over.

'Oh no! Has mum fallen over? Is she OK?'

'No! She's fine, thankfully. It was Daisy's turn for a tumble! I'll go and put the kettle on and rummage around the cake tins and see what I can rustle up. See you soon.'

When I returned to the lounge, Daisy and Mum were discussing the dancing shoe charm. 'Auntie Vanessa was a very good dancer, so was Grandpa, but I had two left feet.' Daisy's eyes opened wide in astonishment and her plump hand covered her mouth, trying to stifle a giggle. Looking firstly at her feet and then at Mum's, she said, 'Poor Grandma.'

Mum laughed 'It's just a saying, love! I've got a left and a right foot just like you!" and proceeded to wiggle them. "Your Auntie Vanessa went in for dancing competitions and won lots of prizes, so Grandpa bought me this charm – shaped like a dancing shoe with a Cuban heel. He was so proud of her. How we used to laugh when I tried to dance.'

The back door opened and in walked Vanessa, 'Dance for us, Auntie, please dance for us!' pleaded Daisy. Looking rather perplexed by this strange greeting,

Vanessa kicked off her wellies, revealing a hole in her sock where her big toe peeped through. Dancing was the last thing on her mind, though – she just flopped into a chair, ready to put her feet up.

Mum looked up and smiled at her younger daughter. She really was the spitting image of Dad's sister, Mabel. Vanessa made herself comfortable in the armchair by the coffee table, and was looking very relaxed by the time I brought in a tray holding a plate of cakes and mugs of tea.

'This is a nice surprise,' said Mum, sighing with deep satisfaction. 'All my favourite girls in one room. How your Dad would have loved this afternoon. It saddens me to think Daisy has so few memories of him.'

Mum picked up the next charm, which was of the Eiffel Tower, 'What a wonderful time we had on this, our last foreign holiday. It was so sad that Dad died a week before our Ruby Wedding anniversary.'

She fingered the charm, as if doing so gave her comfort. 'We had been planning our next trip. We were going to treat ourselves to something special to celebrate,' her voice began to tremble. 'He fancied a cruise, but I wasn't sure I would like it.'

I caught Vanessa's eye and she nodded.

'Mum, when we were helping you sort through Dad's things, we found this box, and with it an anniversary card which he had planned to give you, but we felt it would be too painful to give you on the actual day, so we kept it safe until we felt you would be able to handle it.'

'Here it is, Mum, another token of his love for you.'

I watched Mum take the box in her hand and hesitate, hardly daring to open it. Her hands hovered over the gift, and then she gathered her courage and lifted the lid off the box. Inside was a silver charm, shaped like a half moon.

Daisy peered into the box, 'What does it say on the moon, Granny?' 'It says 'I love you to the moon and back'. Grandpa often said that to me,' and she hugged herself, almost as though she could feel his arms encircling her.

Daisy climbed down out of the chair and ran off into the next room, saying 'I've got a book called that' and immediately returned with it, holding it out to Mum, in the hope that she would read it to her.

Vanessa beckoned Daisy over and patted her lap, indicating she would like to read it. Mum then carefully removed the card from the envelope and, wiping away a tear, opened it up.

In Tom's clumsy handwriting it said, 'To my darling Molly. For the last 40 years you have been the sun and the moon in my life. I was charmed to meet you all those years ago in the bakery, and I have given thanks every day of my life for you. Much love as always, Tom.'

MATEUS

All his life Mateus had felt he was on the outside looking in, and being a window cleaner didn't help in the least. Whatever the time of year, he would peer intently at life on the other side of the glass. Christmas was the worst time for him, when he could see families preparing for the celebrations, gifts piled up by the tree, a time of loving and sharing. He had no one to give to.

Some days his imagination ran riot and he pictured himself with his feet up, lounging on a sumptuous sofa, surrounded by books and glossy magazines, with a brandy in his hand, surveying his wealth like Christopher, the man at Number 42. He had seen him sitting at his bureau, rifling through documents with a disdainful look on his face, seemingly screwing up every third sheet of paper and hurling it at the wastepaper basket – but invariably missing the target. On other occasions he had seen him relaxing, drinking coffee, or reading the paper.

Not all the houses where he cleaned the windows were occupied by happy clients. Polly, the girl at Number 17, with her two snotty-nosed children, certainly didn't have a charmed life. The net curtains were torn and grubby and, as he gazed into her flat, he was aware of the squalor and poverty that surrounded her. The sink was always full of dirty dishes, and soiled nappies overflowed out of a bucket, but he had noticed that recently she seemed to be getting a grip on things and that the children had looked happier in the last couple of months.

Maisie at Number 46 was different. She always had a smile on her face and had time to wave a cheery hello – not just to Mateus, but to anyone who crossed her path. As he polished her windows he felt a warm glow as he looked into her house. The lounge was filled with lots of unusual ornaments and trinkets, and cupboards that she had decorated with decoupage and bright paint. Even her curtains were cheerful – she had made patchwork ones, using scraps of vintage cotton, which gave the room a bohemian feel. He wondered what she did for a job – perhaps she was a teacher or an artist?

As he continued cleaning Maisie's windows he looked into the other rooms for clues. In contrast to the lounge, the bedroom was minimalistic, in muted shades of grey, with clean, simple lines, and just three black and white photos on the wall above the bed. The bathroom was small, with a nautical look, and a vast array of shampoo's and lotions and lotions on the shelf amongst the shells and driftwood. Lastly, the kitchen diner was a fine example of shabby chic, with a painted table and chairs and a polka dot tablecloth.

The final house on his round belonged to Betty, an older lady who seemed vague and forgetful. She was usually sitting in her conservatory when he came, looking out onto her back garden with its fruit trees. In Spring there were red and white tulips in her flower bed, under-planted with blue grape hyacinths and forget me nots, followed by red salvias and blue and white petunias in Summer.

Betty could never remember where her purse was when the time came to pay, and he noticed as time passed that she found it increasingly difficult to give him the right change. She seemed contented and always offered him a coffee and custard cream biscuits. He enjoyed sitting with her in the conservatory and chatting about this and that. He loved her wide vocabulary and the way she used words so expressively. It was a nice way to end the day, before he headed home to his grim bedsit in on the outskirts of town.

The next day was commercial cleaning – the shops in the high street, the small museum, and lastly the library. Mateus enjoyed washing the shop windows almost as much as he did the houses. It left him less room for his fertile imagination but nevertheless there was much to see. In the Sewing Box haberdashery shop a pretty woman of about thirty was rifling through a box of ribbons, turning them over in her hands. Having selected a roll of purple ribbon, she moved onto the button section. The guy from Number 42 was in the off-licence buying some brandy.

Mateus spotted Betty in the supermarket. She was meandering around the aisles, popping various items into her small trolley. Two packets of custard creams were swiftly followed by a brown wholemeal loaf – not the budget version, but an artisan-crafted one, best butter, and an assortment of quality cheeses – Camembert, Stilton, and Boursin.

She wandered through the home-baking section, pausing to look at the food colourings and dainty cake decorations. As she walked down the biscuit aisle she hesitated by the custard creams and picked up another two packets, oblivious to the fact that she already had some in her trolley.

It really was fascinating watching people, getting to know their idiosyncrasies.

Betty was the epitome of the happy shopper. She smiled widely as she approached the meat counter. Money was not a problem for her, she was comfortably off. Her pension from her job as a head teacher was more than adequate, and she had lived with her parents until their deaths, inheriting the house from them. Her retirement present to herself was having a conservatory built – a luxury, but one that gave her great pleasure. Most evenings she would have a glass of wine with her supper, sitting on the rattan sofa. Then she would get out her laptop and work on it for an hour or so.

Mateus continued his observations as he made his way along the High Street, peering in through the shop windows and observing the customers as he washed, wiped and polished the windows. The library would be his last port of call – a large job that usually took a good couple of hours. It was a modern building, light and airy, with a vast expanse of glass to be cleaned. Although it seemed a daunting task for one man, Mateus enjoyed the challenge, and the sense of satisfaction when he had finished the job.

Inside the library there were comfy armchairs and sofas. Gone were the days of silence – now it was a place of bustle and noise. The children's area was a hive of activity, Mums were chatting and drinking coffee, and the librarian sat on the floor reading stories to those who had ears to hear.

Sometimes sessions were run to help people with housing support, employment and financial advice. Many groups met there, including support groups to help those who wanted to give up smoking or drinking, or to get control of their weight, and social groups who met together to share reminiscences, or for creative writing sessions.

Mateus wondered what would be going on today. He knew that there was a support group that met regularly on a Wednesday for the would-be skinnies, where they would talk about food – and sometimes they shared some too. It looked fun, and he thought about his expanding waistline and wondered if he should join in.

As he started washing the windows, he looked into the play area and saw the twins belonging to the girl at Number 17, who had clean faces for once, and were being read to by an older woman. They looked much better here than they had at home – the dinginess of their home surroundings had been shed like a caterpillar's chrysalis, and here they seemed more alert and happier than usual.

A poster on the inside of the glass advertised a creative writing group, Mateus looked at his watch and saw that it had begun ten minutes ago. Just as he was wondering who would go to such a group, the automatic doors opened and Betty walked in, clutching a file of papers and the obligatory custard creams. She looked slightly harassed, and her shoulders were stooped, but when she saw the rest of the regulars she relaxed and took her seat amongst them.

Mateus climbed a little higher up his ladder, so he could see who else was there. They looked like quite a broad mixture of people. The girl from Number 46 had opened her note book and was looking particularly bohemian. He wondered if she always dressed like that, or whether it was part of a writer's persona. She reminded him of a painting by Rossetti – her water-falling auburn hair was swept back, revealing a broad forehead and an aquiline nose. Mateus loved pre-Raphaelite paintings and here was a girl who would have made a fine muse.

It saddened him that, having got a degree in art history, he couldn't find a job to match his qualification, but at least window cleaning was interesting and meant he had a steady income.

His attention was then drawn to the chap from Number 42. He was wearing a Harris tweed jacket that had seen better days and corn-coloured corduroy trousers. The Paisley cravat around his neck gave him a raffish charm. Leaning back in the chair with his hands behind his head he oozed confidence and calm, which wasn't how he had seemed when Mateus had observed him screwing up balls of paper and throwing them into the waste-paper basket.

Mateus was burning with curiosity when he realised that several of his customers were sitting around the table. Normally he would only clean the library windows on the outside, but today he felt compelled to offer to clean them on the inside at no extra charge, just so he could eavesdrop on the writing group.

Once inside the library he leant his ladder against the wall, climbed up it and hovered like a buzzard facing into the wind eyeing up its prey. He could now see over the bookshelves, and below him, at a large table, sat the gathered throng. Interestingly, Polly, the mother of the twins from Number 17, appeared to be in charge. On her iPad she was noting the names of the attendees.

Christopher Soames, the man from Number 42, nodded as she mentioned his name. Maisie Blunt, with her smile as wide as ever, laughed as it reminded her of registration time at school. Betty Sidebottom cringed at the mention of her name. You would have thought at seventy-two she would have been immune to it, but it still bothered her. She had thought of changing it via deed poll to something more acceptable, but it was too much effort.

Polly looked up from her iPad, leant forward and drew her chair in closer to the table, 'Well, how did we all get on with last week's homework?'

Maisie smiled – she was never bothered what others thought about her. 'I found it exhilarating to write about passers-by. I went to the park and loved writing outdoors. It was such a good choice of subject! The sun came out while I was sitting in the park, and the long shadows filled me with delight. Even when the sun had set, its influence was still making its mark.'

Inclining her head toward Chris, she waited for his response to the question. He shuffled in his seat, hunched his shoulders, and looked awkward – more awkward than usual. He asked himself why he put himself through this agony every week 'Well, to be honest, I didn't know where to begin. I'm not very good at this stuff, you know.' he grimaced 'I don't like letting people see what I really think. I feel confused about being emotional, I spend hours trying to write something meaningful, but I chuck most of it into the waste-paper basket, and I can't even get that right. I usually miss the target.'

Betty leant forward and patted him on the arm. 'It's not about how well we do it, Chris, it's about enjoying ourselves.' He recoiled at her touch and withdrew further into himself, like a tortoise into its shell, 'I know, Betty, I know. It's just that I find being retired so difficult – it takes a lot of adjustment. In my job I accomplished so much, and I miss the constant challenge of making people comfortable in uncomfortable circumstances. Success was what I aimed for then, but now I find I can't even write a half-decent short story or a poem.'

Maisie smiled at him, not just with her lips but with her eyes too, 'I've always wondered what you did for a job?' Christopher looked apprehensive, he never talked to anyone about his career, he had even moved to a new town to make a fresh start. Maisie meant well, and he appreciated her concern, but he wasn't sure he wanted to divulge his occupation.

Undertaking wasn't the most glamorous or exciting career choice.

Shuffling in his chair he crossed then uncrossed his legs, 'Er, well…' Polly decided to take charge at this point. 'That's OK, Chris. Whatever you did, I'm sure you did it well. Shall we get on with the task in hand? Last week's homework was to write a poem or short story about someone you passed in the street. Maisie, who did you choose to write about?'

Maisie breathed out, and in her usual gentle, laid-back way began to tell the group about her story. 'Last week I saw this guy in Burton Park, covered in tattoos and with a shaved head. He was stocky, with a face like a pit bull terrier who had swallowed a wasp, but you'll never guess what sort of dog he had – a chihuahua! I wondered what his story was, and I've called my piece 'Storm in a Teacup'.' The group laughed as she regaled them with the tale about the tiny dog called Storm and his interactions with the guy she had named Jeremy. Even Chris managed a weak smile. 'OK, so who's up next?' Chris debated whether to go next and get it over and done with, or to keep quiet, in the hope that they might forget about his contribution.

Mateus wiped off the window he had started and moved onto the next one, even nearer than the group than before. He ascended the ladder and, with his squeegee and scrim in hand, started to wash the window.

Betty's face brightened as she took her turn, 'I've written about my wonderful window cleaner, Mateus. He's such a nice lad! He always makes time to have a chat with me and we enjoy a cup of coffee and a biscuit. Oh yes, would anyone like a custard cream?'

There was the crash of a ladder falling and the clatter of a bucket as Mateus overreached himself. Everyone looked up, wondering what the commotion was. They saw the librarian running from one direction and a student from another. Betty craned her neck and peered between the crime shelves and the biographies where, much to her amazement, she saw Mateus sitting on the floor, looking embarrassed, with the squeegee still in his hand.

'Oh Mateus, are you all right?' she enquired, still trying to make sense of the scene before her. Mateus nodded, grinning sheepishly, his heart beating rapidly, and with a flush of embarrassment on his cheeks. The librarian and the student helped him up and Betty invited him to join them at the table. 'What a coincidence that you should be in the library just as I was about to read my story about you. Would you like to hear it?'

He wasn't too sure that he would, but he didn't want to offend Betty, so he nodded and, rubbing his bruised knee, tried to make himself as comfortable.

Betty cleared her throat and launched into the story. It was a tale of triumph over adversity, of a lonely homesick young Portuguese boy who had come as a student to England to get a degree, knowing no one, and how he struck up an unlikely friendship with a seventy-eight-year-old widow. The quality that she so admired in him was his ability to empathise with people, which made her feel confident and worthy of respect. He never interrupted her when she stumbled over a word, or commented when she lost her purse for the umpteenth time. She felt affirmed by him and strangely strengthened, giving her greater confidence to tackle life's challenges.

For the second time that day he felt humbled, and he twisted the hem of his T-shirt round and round his finger in a distracted way, wanting the ground to swallow him up. As the story drew to a close she patted his arm. 'What a charming lad he is', she told the others. 'He will make someone a wonderful husband someday.' She put the papers down on the table and bit into a custard cream.

Chris felt very relieved that he hadn't been asked to share his yarn about the footballer who never scored a goal. As he rose and left, Polly called after him. 'Oh yes, Chris, next week's homework is to write a story or poem about an undertaker.'

Strangely comforted, he left the library, knowing that this time he really would have something to write about.

GERANIUMS AND GOSSAMER THREADS

The red geraniums seemed to smile at Richard from the window boxes of the Black Cat Café. The sun was shining and the tables and chairs outside looked very inviting, and the smell of coffee and Danish pastries enticed Richard to take a seat outside the café. Not that he needed much encouragement – it was such a pleasant place to while away an afternoon.

Stan, the café owner, came out and took his order. As Richard relaxed, waiting for his coffee to arrive, the earthy scent took his mind went back to happy hours spent with his grandfather in his greenhouse, where his favourite task was watering the geraniums that filled the shelves.

This thought quickly followed by another one, a seemingly random memory that just popped into his head. 'Smell this flower, Richard. Have a really good sniff.' He remembered leaning forward and inhaled deeply, 'It's tickling my nose, Grandpa!' There, in the greenhouse all those years ago, was the moment Richard's love of gardening was born.

'I grow these especially for Granny, as her name is Lily, and that's what these flowers are called too. They are my favourite, as they make me think how much I love her, but she likes roses best. I grow her lots of those, so she can pick them and have them in vases in the house.'

Inside the house an arrangement of flowers always stood on the sideboard, lovingly chosen by Grandpa and expertly arranged by Granny. In the winter, on his half day from the shop, Grandpa would pop into the florist and buy a bunch of something cheerful, to brighten up the lounge and remind them that spring was approaching.

Stan returned with a latte and a vanilla slice. As Richard picked it up, he lingered before taking the first mouthful of the cake, and recalled his grandmother taking him to a very high-class shop in town, where mouth-watering cream cakes were their speciality. You had to go upstairs, taking great care as you walked through the china department, but once on the upper floor the smell of homemade cakes and tea attracted you like moths to a flame. He remembered gazing into the glass cabinet where all manner of sweet delights almost danced before his eyes.

'Now Richard, which one would you like?' his grandmother asked. Oh, the agony of deciding. With his nose pressed against the glass he eventually whittled it down to a choice of two – a meringue swan or a vanilla slice – the latter winning as it looked bigger! He remembered feeling so grown up, and then the sensation of the cream oozing out onto his chin and Granny leaning forward and wiping it off with her hankie. Did everyone's mothers and grandmothers spit on their hankies before wiping children's faces?

Back to the present he took his first bite, the flaky pastry melting in his mouth. Looking up he saw Kate heading towards the café with Freda. He liked Kate – she reminded him a bit of his daughter Sally, with her bohemian clothes and caring manner. He knew Freda had been feeling under the weather and worried about her memory, so it pleased him to see them walking together in the late summer sunshine.

Relaxing back in his chair and sipping his latte he looked up and down the street, enjoying the gentle pace of life in this quiet market town. Mothers were pushing babies in their buggies, an old man was wheeling his wife in a wheelchair, the cycle of life was always turning.

A gentle breeze carried the aroma of coffee to him, and he was instantly transported back to the café in Giverny where he and Elizabeth had spent their silver wedding anniversary, eavesdropping on the conversations of young lovers and students, as people-watching had become one of their favourite pastimes. Nestled together on a bench between the trees in Monet's garden, they enjoyed the scent of the rambling roses scrambling over the walls, before setting off to admire the iconic vistas created by Monet himself.

Elizabeth's favourite view was of the Japanese bridge spanning the lake. She felt that Monet was in tune with nature and she always found this to be a healing place. Whatever season they went to visit, she always had a sense of harmony and reconciliation in the beautiful garden.

Leaning back in his chair outside the cafe a distant unfocused smile spread across Richard's face as he thought about his own garden. Together he and Sally had recreated in a small way the scene at Giverny. Seeing a wooden bridge for sale at a garden centre on one of their outings, impulsively he bought it and had it delivered to the house. With a friend Alan, a local gardener, a pond was created and the bridge put in place. Something seemed lacking – it didn't make enough of a statement – so Alan and Sally moved it back onto the grass and while Richard decided what to do.

A visit to Clyne Gardens in Swansea came to mind, and he was sure that he had seen a red bridge there. He asked Sally to find the photos she had taken of their holiday and sure enough, in contrast to the greenery, the bridge looked magnificent. Richard got some pillar box red paint and the transformation was completed.

Enthusiasm swept them away and together they laid a winding path, symbolic of life's journey, leading to a bench, painted the same brilliant red, which was placed at the far corner of the garden. It drew the eye and gave a new sense of perspective – an invitation to see the garden from a different view. It also was somewhere to rest their weary bodies after working hard, and somewhere to relax and read with a glass of wine. What fun they had planting vibrant red maples and bamboo, camellias and hostas.

No expense was spared when it came to the garden and Richard knew in his heart of hearts that Elizabeth would have been so thrilled, not just to be remembered in such a personal way, but also that he and Sally – both artists – had bonded creatively.

Looking down at his empty plate and then at his watch he rose from the table, paid his bill and set off for home. As he entered the garden he noticed a spider's web tenuously attached to a geranium, glistening in the sunlight. Pausing, he admired its delicate weaving and then continued round to the back of the house, where he found Sally relaxing on the bench. She put her book down and got up to greet him, 'Have you had a good afternoon Dad? Tell me all about it, where did you go?'

'I popped into the library and then sat in the sun outside the Black Cat Café. I saw Freda and what's her name? Begins with N, I think'

'Kate?'

'Yes, I told you it began with an N!' he laughed.

'Did you have something nice to eat at the café?'

'Yes, I had … er, I had …,' Richard paused, trying hard to remember what he had just eaten. 'No, no good, it's gone. I thought about your mother and my grandmother, it's most annoying that I can remember things from sixty years ago but not what I ate sixty minutes ago.'

Glancing at the geraniums he looked again at the spider's web with its gossamer threads flimsily spanning the gap between the rose and its stem, and thought how delicate life can seem at times. But even if one thread breaks away from the web, this failure doesn't prevent it functioning.

'Seems a bit like my brain really,' he smiled to himself.

Comforted by that thought, he ambled off into the house to make a cup of tea and listen to the radio.

THE MEMORY BOX

Richard De La Roche lifted the lid of the box and smiled in delight at its contents.

Sally, his daughter, smiled too as she watched his face. She guided his arthritic hands, liver-spotted by many hours gardening in the sun, towards a packet of seeds that nestled between a gardening glove and a faded photograph of a boy watering plants in a conservatory.

'Do you know what seeds these are, Dad?' Sally asked.

'Sweet peas. I used to grow them for your mother'.

Sally's relationship with her father was now on an even keel, but it had been stormy in the past. One of the moments that marked their new understanding had been when he acknowledged the increasing frailty of his body and asked her to plant out his precious sweet peas. It was a job he always relished, but the time had come to let her loose in the garden and acknowledge that her love of gardening had woven their lives together.

Now she wasn't just his daughter, but also his carer, his comforter and his friend.

When her mother Elizabeth had died, Sally had thought long and hard about how to build a relationship with her irascible father, and it had occurred to her that the common ground in their lives was that they both had a garden. Years later this bond between them was stronger than ever.

Had she suggested 'Let's make a memory box', he would have insisted that his memory was perfect, so Sally just appeared with it one winter's morning when it was too cold to go out for a walk.

He put the seed packet back into the box and picked out the photo of the boy, with his neatly cut fringe and immaculate white shirt, who was expertly applying water to coleus and heliotrope, 'Mmm, I can remember the delicious perfume of cherry pie as I watered the heliotrope.'

Smells were important to him and a waft of someone wearing Chanel No. 5 would transport him back to meeting Elizabeth for the first time on the commuter train to London, and as their relationship grew, the dinner-dances they attended, where she would dress up for the occasion.

Sally still used the same aluminium watering can as the one in the photo, which was next to the water butt ready for action, just outside the back door. It had seen better days, but then so had they both.

'I can remember you Sally picking up the Chanel perfume box when you had just learnt to read and asking your mother why she wore 'Channel No 5', and how she had laughed.' He thought of the conservatory, which ran the length of the house, and was filled with plants that were popular in the 1930's. A multitude of geraniums in various hues, all grown by his father, were resplendent on the wooden shelves, benefiting from the summer sun.

A miniature garden gnome then caught his eye and he took it out of the box and smiled at it.

This gnome, with its white beard, had been given to him last year on his birthday by Sally. It had become a tradition that every year she would give him something with a label attached which read 'I saw this and thought of you!' He stroked his beard as he held the gnome. One year she had bought him a pastry brush like a cockatiel, because its Mohican haircut reminded her of the tufty bits that grew on his balding head, and another year a box containing a preparation to cure farting in bed. This spoof medication had caused much hilarity between them as he always blamed the dog for any unfortunate odours, irrespective of who had made them.

He returned the gnome and the photo to the box and removed with shaking hands another black and white photograph, this time of himself at the seaside with his grandmother Louisa, his mother Win, and her cousin Elsie.

The formal dresses which the women wore hardly looked suitable for a day at the beach. Richard studied himself and noticed, clutched in his right hand, a metal beach spade.

Sally had scanned the original tiny photo then enlarged and laminated it so Richard could see it more clearly. His left hand at first glimpse appeared to be holding the hand of this elegant cousin, dressed in white. He looked pleased to be seen with her – even from an early age he had admired women who dressed well. On closer inspection, he was actually holding the hand of a Mickey Mouse doll and Elsie was on the other end of it, uniting in his fantasy. Elsie's fashionable two-tone shoes were such a contrast to his mother's sensible pair.

Richard commented 'I loved my mother dearly, with her round tortoiseshell glasses and ample figure. She was no show stopper, but her wisdom, tenderness, and unconditional love were far more valuable than skin-deep looks. I can almost smell the ozone, and feel the warmth of the sun, and the taste of the salt in the air.'

He returned to the present and peered at the treasure trove. His eyes fell on a smaller box containing a jigsaw, with a picture of Monet's waterlilies on the front. He knew his shaking fingers would struggle with the jigsaw pieces, but with Sally's help they would be able to complete it.

It was the same with his garden – he knew what he wanted to do, but needed Sally's hands to put it into action. Monet's garden was his little indulgence, and when time and money permitted he had travelled by coach to Giverny, where he had paid homage to this master gardener. He regretted not having included Sally in these excursions, but it was too late for regrets. His adventurous travelling days were done, but trips to a nearby garden centre, or a walk along the pier, still gave them both great pleasure.

His own garden, like Monet's, was created with an artistic eye. He and Sally had together created a Japanese garden with a red bridge, which was a source of much delight when they looked at it out of the kitchen window when they did the washing up together.

Sally had never really measured up to his expectations in so many ways. She was other-worldly, preferring simplicity over wealth. Her hippy clothes annoyed him, but she was a fiercely loyal daughter and was doing all she could to make his life as pleasant and positive as possible.

As his hand reached for another object from the box she put her rough, work-worn hand on his, and together they took out a CD – today it was Vivaldi's Four Seasons. They shared a love of music and would relax back into the comfort of the sofa and enjoy listening side by side.

The memory box had been her idea, and she felt rewarded by the waterfall of hidden memories and emotions which came cascading out each time he opened the box. Sometimes he would ask where the box was, and she would get it out so that they could spend time together, allowing him to reminisce. She cherished the opportunity to learn more about her father and their family. From time to time Sally would change the photos, tracking down pictures of places that Richard mentioned, in the hope of recovering more happy reminiscences. As new stories came to mind she would adapt the contents of the memory box.

Sweet peas would be replaced by cosmos; the gnome would be swapped with a pastry brush to remind him of Elizabeth's cooking; and after they had listened to the Vivaldi disc she would swap it for a Rogers and Hammerstein. They might even sing together some songs from Carousel, knowing that he loved to tell the story of how he and Elizabeth had been given tickets to the opening night at Drury Lane as a wedding present. She would include a photograph of Elizabeth holding their Dachshund puppy, who they called Julie Jordan, after the main character in the musical.

The next time he lifted the lid, he would open up different memories. Sally was looking forward to learning more about her father's earlier life. The memory box was giving them a connection across time, and bringing them closer in a very special way.

ABOUT THE AUTHOR

Sarah Veness is eager to empower people to live life to the full. Writing from her own experience she aims to bring insight to help those particularly with memory problems and their carers.

A stroke survivor, she lives by the motto 'Don't curse the darkness – light a candle.'

Trained as a Dementia Champion, she also gives talks on how to make memory books and boxes and is a prize winning photographer and artist. In her spare time she loves gardening, being creative and relaxing with friends.

She was winner of the inaugural Literature Works Primary Carers Voice short story competition and shortlisted in The Alzheimer's Society Poetry Award.

You can find out more about her on her blog cookingbykindlelight.wordpress.com

30365871R00045

Printed in Poland
by Amazon Fulfillment
Poland Sp. z o.o., Wrocław